W9-AJW-049

Disney Moana

The Mighty Maui Makes a Friend

By
Kalikolehua Hurley

Illustrated by
Mehrdad Isvandi

A special thanks to the wonderful people of the **PACIFIC ISLANDS** for inspiring us on this journey as we bring the world of Moana to life.

To my mom, the mightiest of them all. And to my love, CLK.

-KH

I dedicate this book to my wife, Sara, for all her support.

-MI

Designed by Tony Fejeran

Printed in the United States of America

First Hardcover Edition, February 2017 10 9 8 7 6 5 4 3 2 1

ISBN 978-1-4847-8292-7

FAC-03427-17006

Library of Congress Control Number: 2016953972

For more Disney Press fun, visit www.disneybooks.com

For more Moana fun, visit www.disney.com/moana

Let me tell you a story about the mighty Maui.

You've heard of him, right?

Half man,

half myth.

ALL HERO.

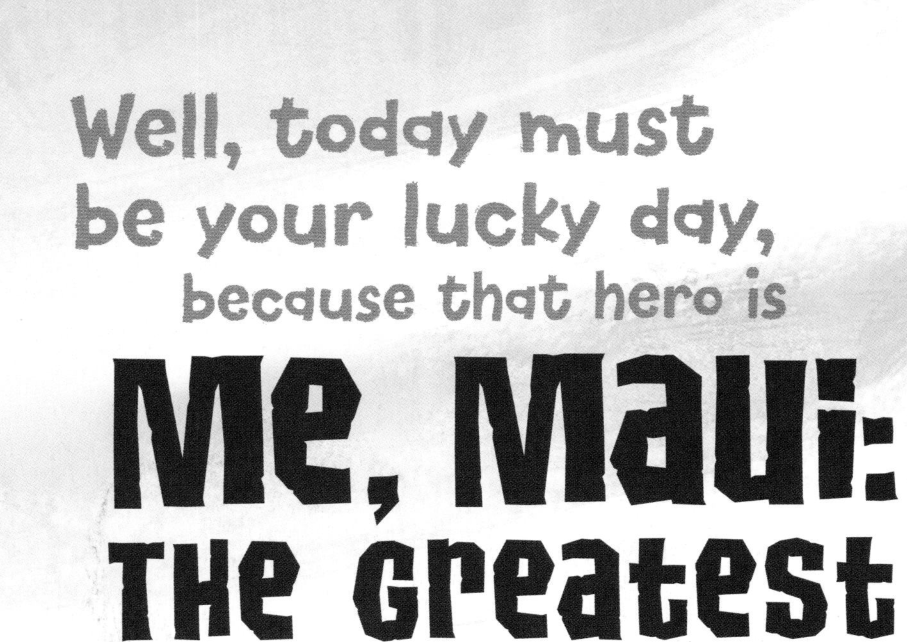

Well, today must
be your lucky day,
because that hero is

ME, MAUI:
THE GREATEST

demigod in the Pacific. With my
magical fishhook, I've done

INCREDIBLE
THINGS.

I PUSHED UP
the sky so humans could walk upright.

I SLOWED DOWN the sun

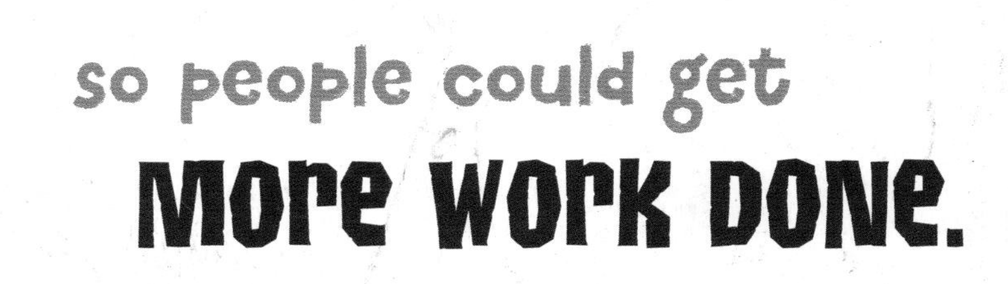

so people could get **MORE WORK DONE.**

I captured

wind

and fire.

I pulled up

islands . . .

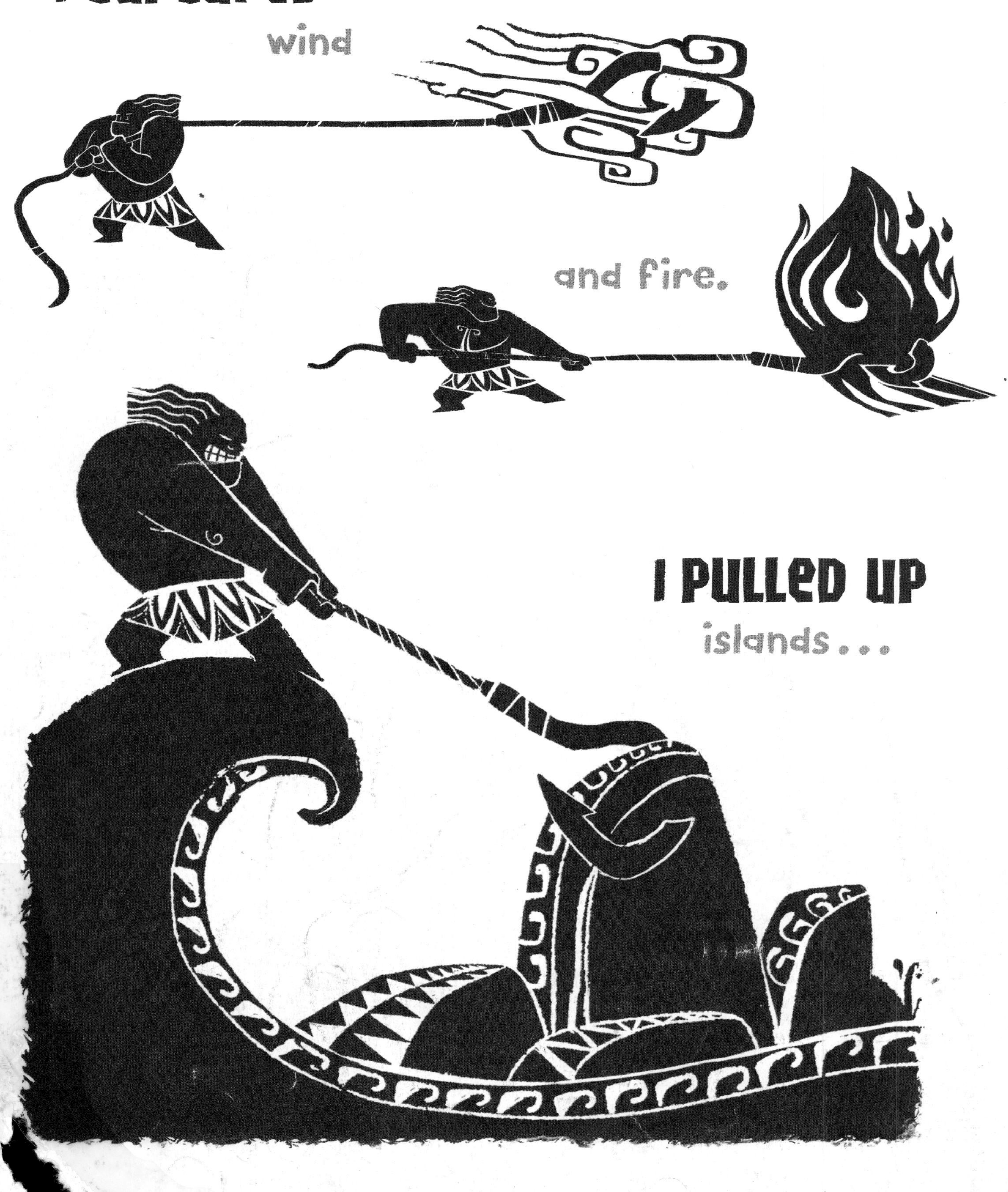

and even helped **create** coconuts!

Yeah,

you're welcome.

Oh, and I can also change my shape.

Supercool

SHARK?

Coming right up.

awesome gigantic hawk?

Thought you'd never ask.

Itsy-bitsy also

awesome bug

Done!  So watch wher

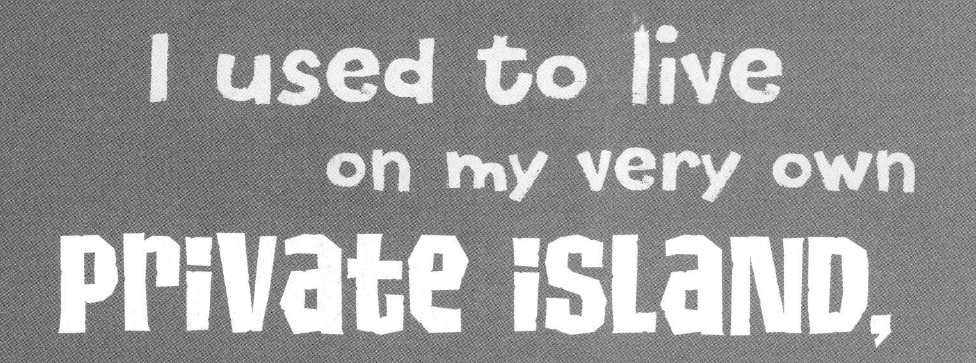
I used to live
on my very own
PRIVATE ISLAND,

ALL
BY
MYSELF!

Being alone wasn't so bad. I didn't have to share my dinner. I could tell myself my favorite story **a MILLION times.**

(PS: It was about me.)

But one day, I realized there was one
thing the mighty Maui had yet to do:

BE A FRIEND. . . .

Then Moana showed up, and it was

Maui Friendship time!

Naturally, I became an expert at being **a FRIEND.**

And I found out some of friendship's most mysterious rules right away.

For example, it turns out friends have to be **NICE** to each other.

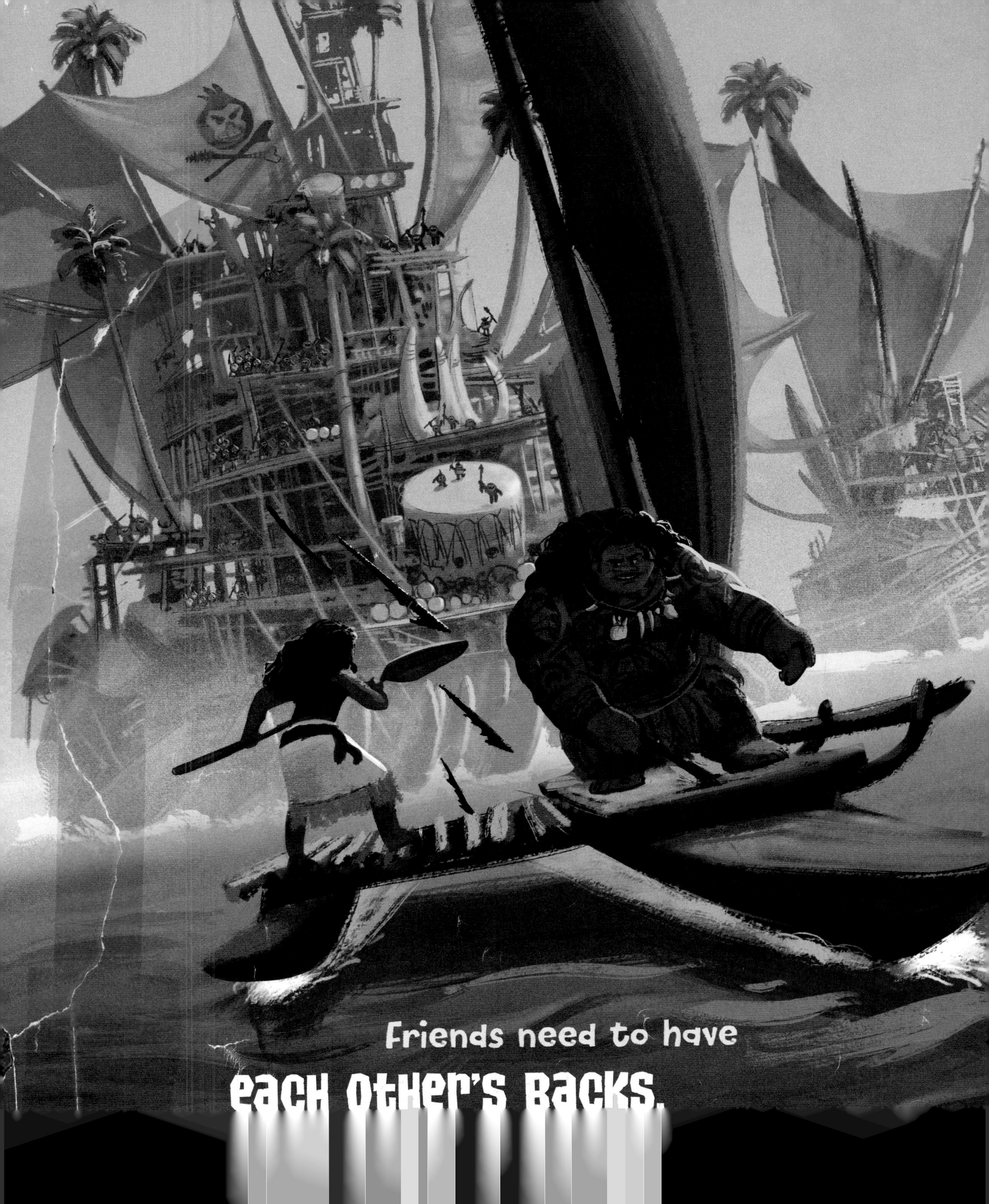
Friends need to have
each other's backs.

And when the going gets tough,
friends never, ever leave each other
STRANDED.

In no time, I was becoming the greatest friend of all time.

You see, friends teach each other new things—like me teaching Moana how to be the world's

SECOND-BEST WAYFINDER.

Friends share.

Hey, when you're a master fisherman, you can spare a fish or two.

Friends listen.

Between us, even a demigod who has experienced it all can discover something new.

Having a friend means you've got someone to

CHEER YOU ON.

It also means you have someone who accepts

YOU FOR YOU.

I learned that from Moana.

Moana and I,
together as friends,
went on an epic adventure
and basically **saved**
the world.

And the mighty Maui finally added

FRIENDSHIP

to his list of feats.

Thanks for listening to my story.
Now you can call yourself
MY
FRIEND,
too.